Max's sister, Ruby, saved up a walletful of money for Grandma's birthday present.

"We're going to buy Grandma a music box with skating ballerinas, Max," said Ruby. "Get your lucky quarter and let's go shopping!"

Ruby took one dollar

from her wallet to pay the bus fare.

The bus stopped at Rosalinda's Gift Shop.

In the window was a music box with skating ballerinas.

"Isn't it beautiful, Max!" said Ruby.

"Thirsty," said Max.

"You may buy a very, very small lemonade, Max," said Ruby.

Next door in Candi's Corner window were hundreds of
vampire teeth.

Max knew Grandma would love a set of teeth with oozing
cherry syrup inside for her birthday.

He bought them instead of the lemonade.

"Two dollars, please," said Candi.

Max wanted to make sure the teeth worked.

He put them in.

The teeth worked perfectly.

Ruby had to take Max to the Laundromat.

It was lunchtime.

Max finished off a peanut butter and jelly sandwich,

two coconut cupcakes,   and a banana shake.

Lunch cost four dollars.

"Money is running through our fingers, Max," said Ruby.

They walked all the way back to Rosalinda's Gift Shop without spending another penny.

"I'd like to buy the music box with skating ballerinas for
Grandma's birthday," Ruby said to Rosalinda.

"It's a hundred dollars," said Rosalinda.

"A hundred dollars!" said Ruby.

"The ice skates are made of real gold," Rosalinda explained.

Ruby looked in her wallet. The only thing left was a five-dollar bill.

"Here's an idea!" said Rosalinda. "Bluebird earrings that play
'Oh, What a Beautiful Morning!' are on sale for four dollars. Gift
wrap is free."

"We'll take them," said Ruby.

Ruby gave Rosalinda the five-dollar bill

for the bluebird earrings

and went to pick out wrapping paper.

"Four dollars for the earrings . . . one dollar change!" said
Rosalinda. "You take care of this dollar, young man!"

Max went back to Candi's Corner. Glow-in-the-dark vampire
teeth were half price.

"Most people like Glow-in-the-dark vampire teeth much better
than the oozing cherry kind," said Candi.

Max bought a set

for one dollar.

"Oh, no, Max," said Ruby. "You've spent our last dollar.

How are we going to pay for the bus home?"

Max reached into his pocket. Out came his lucky quarter.
Ruby used it for the telephone.

"Grandma will have to pick us up," said Ruby. "I hope she
won't be angry."

Grandma was not angry at all.

She was so thrilled, she played the musical bluebird earrings

and wore the vampire teeth all the way home.

Making Money!

If you want to go shopping with Max and Ruby,

you will need plenty of Bunny Money.

Ask a grown-up to help you photocopy the money

that is inside the front and back covers of this book.

Then, with a grown-up's help, cut out

the money you have photocopied and

paste the fronts to the backs

(plain sides together).

You can color your money

if you like.

Happy shopping!

JONAS SALK

MOTHER HALE

MAHATMA GANDHI

YO-YO MA

JESSYE NORMAN

MARIE CURIE

MARTINA NAVRATILOVA

JULIA CHILD